by *Elizabeth Dale*

illustrated by *Alan Marks*

ORCHARD BOOKS

To Caroline, with love

Text copyright © 1998 by Elizabeth Dale
Illustrations copyright © 1998 by Alan Marks
First American edition 1998 published by Orchard Books
First published in Great Britain in 1998 by Ragged Bears Limited

Orchard Books, 95 Madison Avenue, New York, NY 10016

Manufactured in Hong Kong   Book design by Mina Greenstein
The text of this book is set in 20 point Sabon.
The illustrations are watercolor.   10 9 8 7 6 5 4 3 2 1

Library of Congress cataloging is available upon request.

ISBN 0-531-30101-X   LC 98-9317

How Long?

"Mommy?" asked Caroline.
"How long before you can
come and read me a story?"

"Oh, in a minute,"
said her mother.

But how long was
a minute?

Caroline didn't know.
So she kept on painting
and painting.

"Here I am!" said her mother.

Caroline looked at her
painting.

That long!

"Mommy!" cried Caroline.
"How long until lunch?"

"Oh, about ten minutes,"
said her mother.

But how long
was ten minutes?
Caroline didn't know.
So she lined up her trucks.

"Lunch is ready!"
called her mother.

Caroline looked at her
long line of trucks.

That long!

"Mommy!" called Caroline.
"How long until you can play
with me?"

"Oh, about fifteen minutes,"
said her mother.

But how long was fifteen minutes?
Caroline didn't know. So she
kept on digging in the sand.

"I'm ready now!"
called her mother.

Caroline looked at her great
long tunnel.

That long!

"Mommy!" called Caroline.
"How long until the moon
comes out?"

"Oh, about twenty
minutes," said her mother.

But how long was twenty
minutes?
Caroline didn't know.
So she kept on making
her daisy chain.

"The moon is coming out now," called her mother.

Caroline looked at her daisy chain.

That long!

After supper, Caroline's mother
asked her to tidy up. "You've got
twenty minutes until bedtime!"
she said. "So don't be long!"

Caroline smiled and looked at
her daisy chain. Twenty
minutes was a long time.
So she started playing
with her trucks . . . and
her paints . . . and
her sandpile. . . .

And then, suddenly,
it was bedtime.

"Come on Caroline, I'll help you tidy up," said her mother. "It's been a long day."

Caroline looked at her painting, her trucks, her sand tunnel, and her daisy chain.

"It has been a *very* long day!" she said, yawning.

She cuddled with her mother as
they snuggled in their nest.
"I do love you Mommy,"
said Caroline.

"I love you too," said her
mother.

"How long will you love me for?"
asked Caroline.

"Oh," said her mother as they
looked up at the night sky.
"As long as it took to make all
the stars in the sky and the moon
and everything else there is."

"That long!" said Caroline.
That was a very long time.
"And then will you stop
loving me?" she asked.

"Oh no," her mother replied.
"After all that long time,
I will have only just begun!"